CLARA'S DANCING FEET

Jean Richardson and Joanna Carey

G.P. Putnam's Sons   New York

I would like to thank
Shirley Grahame and her dancing school
for starting me off on the right foot.
JR

Text copyright © 1986 Jean Richardson
Illustrations copyright © 1986 Joanna Carey
First American edition 1987
First published by Methuen Children's Books Ltd,
London, England.

Library of Congress Cataloging-in-Publication Data

Richardson, Jean.
   Clara's dancing feet.

Summary: Clara longs to take dancing lessons, but when
she arrives in class, her feet refuse to move.
[1. Dancing—Fiction] I. Carey, Joanna. II. Title.
PZ7.R39485C1 1987   [E]   86-8143
ISBN 0-399-21388-0
First impression

Printed in Hong Kong by South China Printing Co.

for Clara Emily Wittmann
when she grows up
JR

for F. S. de M. C.
JC

Clara, small and bouncy as a rubber ball, loved to dance.
All kinds of music went straight to her feet. She would be
a rock star in the kitchen, a tap dancer in the hall, and a
little swan in the living room.

"Not in here, Clara," her mother would say.

"Go away," her brother would say. "I'm doing my
homework."

Even the cat didn't appreciate Clara's dancing.

One day Emily came to play.
She had just moved in next
door. Clara and Emily were
the same age.

"I can do lots of things,"
Emily said. "I can skip. I can
skate. I can dance. And I can
play the flute. What can
you do?"

Clara wasn't sure she liked
Emily, but she was impressed.
She wasn't very good at
skipping, and she couldn't
skate or play the flute.

What could she do? "I can
dance," she told Emily.
"Show me."
So Clara stood on tiptoe and
fluttered her arms like wings.

"That's not real dancing," Emily said. "You have to do positions for real dancing. Like this." And she put her heels together and turned out her toes until her feet were in a straight line, just like a ballerina.

Clara couldn't see what this had to do with dancing, but she tried to put her feet in a straight line — and fell over.

"That's because you haven't had lessons," Emily explained. "You have to have lessons if you want to be a real dancer."

Clara asked her father if she could take dancing lessons.
Then Clara asked her mother.

"It's a little late for this year," her mother told her.
"School is almost over."

But Clara had made up her mind. She wanted to dance. *Now.* Not next year.

Finally, her mother said, "We'll go and talk to the teacher."

Mrs Lightbody looked at Clara's feet and legs and made her walk up and down. "Nothing wrong there," she said.

"We only have three more classes,
but perhaps Clara would like to come
and see what we've learned
so far."
   She gave Clara's
mother a
list of things
Clara would need
for her classes.

Clara had never seen anywhere like *Pirouette*.
They had everything from stiff white ballet
skirts to rock-and-roll jump suits — all for
dancing.

She would have liked striped leg warmers,
but the list said a white leotard, a pink sweater
and white socks. She fell instantly in love with
the satin ballet shoes, which made her feet
look like two sugared almonds.

Clara was the first to arrive at the dancing school on
Thursday. She put on her leotard, her socks and her ballet
shoes. Clara's mother braided her hair and pinned it up
on top of her head.

Then Emily and the others arrived.
Suddenly, Clara felt shy.

When they were dressed, everyone went into the next room. Except Clara. She followed behind and stopped in the doorway.

Most of the class, especially Emily, were racing around the room.

"In the middle of the room, please," Mrs Lightbody called. "Make a circle." The children ran together and held hands. All except Clara.

She stayed in the doorway. Something had happened to her feet. Or was it her legs? They wouldn't move.

"Come along, Clara." Mrs Lightbody held out her hand. Clara longed to run and join the circle, but her feet were stuck to the floor. Its golden wood, so springy to dance on, held her fast, like toffee.

"All right," Mrs Lightbody said, kindly. "You stay there and watch."

So Clara stayed where she was. The piano was played by a lady who looked like her grandmother. All the music came out of her head. She had tunes for pointing toes, bouncy tunes for skipping, and fast tunes for galloping.

And when she wasn't playing, she knitted.

"Stand up nice and straight," Mrs Lightbody said. "Pretend you're a puppet with strings pulling you up to the ceiling. Can you feel them?"

She put a stool in the middle of the floor and told the class it was a tall Christmas tree and they were fairies with wands who had to light the candles on it.

Emily's tiptoes wobbled, and George lost his balance and knocked over the stool.

Then it was time for skipping and galloping. "Off you go," the music said, and Emily held out her hand to Clara, but Clara couldn't move.

"What happened, Clara?" her mother asked, when they got home. "All that fuss about wanting to dance, and then you wouldn't join in."

Clara couldn't explain why. But when her mother was busy in the kitchen and her brother was upstairs doing his homework, she put on her ballet shoes and tried the steps she had seen in class.

She pointed her toes, she turned them out, she bobbed up and down, bending her knees. Then she galloped around, leading first with one foot, then the other, the way Emily had done.

Even the cat seemed impressed. "You see, I *can* dance," she told him.

But the next week the same thing happened. Clara
wanted to dance, but she just couldn't do it. It was like
the time she had climbed to the top of the big slide in the
park and had been too frightened to let go. Then the boy
behind her had pushed her.

"Don't worry," Mrs Lightbody said. "Next week is our last class and the parents will be coming to see our performance. You come too and watch."

That day, Clara sat with the audience. She wasn't wearing her leotard or her ballet shoes.

The class came out waving reins of scarlet ribbons as they pranced around like circus ponies, stamping their hooves and tossing their heads to the music.

Clara found it irresistible. She forgot about being shy.
She forgot she wasn't wearing her leotard and ballet shoes.

She forgot about the parents watching. She ran across the floor and joined the ponies.

One, two, three, went the piano. One, two, three,

went Clara, keeping pace with the others. Everyone was looking at her, but it didn't matter. She was a real dancer, at last.

"Well," Mrs Lightbody said to Clara when it was over,
"that was some debut! I hope you'll come to classes next
year and learn all the other steps too."

"Yes, please," Clara said. And she looked down at her
grey socks and wriggled her toes. She knew that next
time her feet wouldn't refuse to dance.